THE PEANUT-BUTTER
BURGLARY

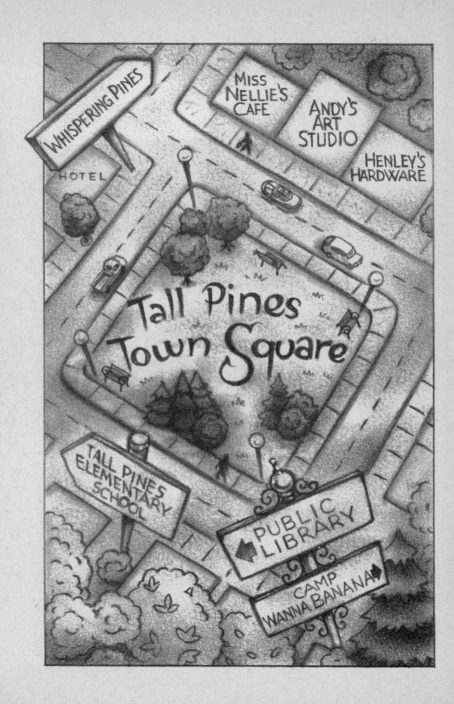

CAMP WANNA BANANA MYSTERIES

THE PEANUT-BUTTER BURGLARY

Becky Freeman

WaterBrook
PRESS

THE PEANUT-BUTTER BURGLARY
PUBLISHED BY WATERBROOK PRESS
2375 Telstar Drive, Suite 160
Colorado Springs, Colorado 80920
A division of Random House, Inc.

The characters and events in this book are fictional, and any resemblance to actual persons or events is coincidental.

ISBN 1-57856-352-6

Published in association with the literary agency of Alive Communications, Inc., 7680 Goddard Street, Suite 200, Colorado Springs, CO 80920.

Printed in the United States of America
2002—First Edition

10 9 8 7 6 5 4 3 2 1

To my fun nephew Tyler,
who loves Blue Bell ice cream,
fishing for bass,
laughing out loud,
and reading good mysteries!

CONTENTS

Acknowledgments ix

1   Pantry Thief 1

2   Cat Burglar? 11

3   Not the Usual Suspects 17

4   Peanut-Butter Clues 27

5   Runaways 33

6   Putting Four Heads Together 41

7   Hot Off the Press 45

8   Marco's Big Idea 49

9   Back-Room Investigation 53

10   Hideaway Home 57

11   Intruders! 63

12   Back to Life 67

13   Goin' to the Cabin-Chapel of Love 73

The Twiblings' Activity Pages 77

ACKNOWLEDGMENTS

Gratitude to Erin Healy, the world's best editor; Greg Johnson, the world's best agent; and my husband and kids, the best family a "crazy" writing woman could ask for! Also to Stephen Arterburn for his enthusiasm for this project, to the WaterBrook and Children of Faith gang, and to David Austin Clar for the terrific artwork that brings the Camp Wanna Banana characters to life. Finally, to the Creator of All, for the gift of imagination and storytelling!

1

PANTRY THIEF

Marco Garcia walked out of Tall Pines Elementary School and shaded his dark eyes against the bright springtime sun. His eyes caught Chad Riggs, a new kid in school, riding off on a brand-new, bright blue mountain bike toward Whispering Pines Estates, where the fanciest houses in Tall Pines were built. Chad was wearing the most popular (and most expensive) brand of jeans and basketball shoes. Marco felt a twinge of jealousy wash over him. *Some kids just seem to have everything.*

Marco turned to his twin sister, Maria, who was walking beside him. "I wonder what it would be like to be able to have anything you wanted," he said.

Maria nodded and smiled. She hugged her books to her chest and asked, "What would you buy?"

Marco thought a minute. "A mountain bike like Chad's, to start with." He ran his fingers through his thick black hair until it stood up crazily. "And cool tennis shoes to replace these ratty old ones. Then I'd buy Mama and Papa a red Corvette so they wouldn't have to drive that rickety ranch truck everywhere. And I'd buy us all a big house—one with white columns and lots of big rooms and fancy furniture. My room would be *huge* with space to spread out and watch my own cable TV and play video games and do research on my high-speed computer."

"Hmmm," answered Maria thoughtfully, absent-mindedly twisting a strand of her long dark hair. "It would be fun to have all that stuff, but I like our little house at Camp Wanna Banana. I think our attic bedrooms are like cozy squirrels' nests. What *I'd* really like is to be able to buy all the books I wanted, anytime I wanted to buy them!"

Marco shook his head. Maria and her friend, Joy,

were always talking about books, books, books. Not that Marco didn't enjoy a good book as much as the next kid. But he wasn't at all interested in the sissy girl stuff his sister liked: *Little House on the Prairie, Anne of Green Gables, American Girl.* Yuck!

"Yeah," said Marco, "I'd buy all the books I could read on how things work. You know, the human body, stars, plants, animals, machines…"

"You really like medicine and science and stuff, don't you?" Maria asked.

"Yep."

"Think you'll be a doctor or scientist someday?"

"I don't know," Marco answered seriously. "I might just continue my work as an ace detective. It allows me to use the great variety of stored-up knowledge in my brain."

Maria laughed out loud. Marco frowned. Ever since Marco and his best buddy, Jake Bigsley (who was also Joy's twin brother), decided to form the Dos Amigos Detective Agency last year, it seemed to him that Maria and Joy never took them seriously.

Just then, Jamie Klem came running up to the twins, breathless, her blond braids flying behind her. Jamie and her big family of ten had moved to Arizona from Georgia last fall in time for the new school year. Marco loved listening to her Southern accent. He could hardly believe real people talked like she did!

"Hey, y'all, Miss Nellie's got chocolate peanut-buttuh ice cream todaaay," Jamie drawled sweetly. "Jake and Joah are waitin' for you at the café. They told me to run tell y'all to hurry up on ovah befoah it's all gone!"

"Thanks, Jaaaaime," Marco answered, playfully trying to mimic the way Jamie stretched out her words. But she didn't even seem to notice; she was already on her way back to Miss Nellie's Café.

Marco and Maria walked the two blocks from school over to Tall Pines's town square in front of Miss Nellie's place. Her popular café was on a corner of the square. Miss Nellie, a pretty lady in her thirties, kept long benches outside in front of the glass windows to the café, where old folks could "set a spell" or young kids could sit and wait for their rides home from school if they weren't riding the bus. Next to the café was Andy's Art Studio. The shades were drawn, and a hand-printed sign on the locked door read, "Gone to Texas to visit the grandkids. Will reopen June 1. See you then!" On the other side of the art studio, at the end of the small block, was Henley's Hardware.

Because both sets of twins lived near each other, their parents often took turns carpooling the Twiblings, as Mrs. Bigsley called the foursome, back and forth to school, church, and sports activities. The Garcias and Bigsleys worked odd jobs during Camp Wanna Banana's off-season to make ends meet, but most days at least one of them was able to pick up the kids after school. Today, Mr. Garcia would pick up the foursome after shoeing a neighboring rancher's horses, but he would be about twenty minutes late. The twins never minded when their parents ran late, especially if it meant time for ice cream at Miss Nellie's. Their parents never worried about them in the quiet little town of Tall Pines, where good-hearted (if sometimes nosy) townspeople watched over the square near the school. In fact, Marco's mother would often say, "In a small town, if you don't know what you're doing, you can be sure everyone else does!"

Marco glanced at his watch. *Just enough time to go in for a scoop!* he thought cheerfully.

Marco glanced at the café window and noticed several colorful country quilts, a rocker, and a couple of hay bales arranged in front of a sign that said, "Come on in, put your feet up, and enjoy today's homemade goodies!" Miss Nellie changed the window display every month. "I like to keep the place bright and interesting," she would say. "Keeps the customers curious—and coming back for seconds!" Miss Nellie was the most energetic businesswoman in town and one of the nicest grownups Marco had ever met.

He paused to open the door for Maria and nodded to Mr. Henley, who was coming out of Miss Nellie's place with his orange tabby cat, Pumpkin. The pet acted more like a dog than a cat, gallantly padding out the door behind her owner, who was headed back to his hardware store.

As Marco and Maria entered the cool shop, they heard a commotion of conversation going on behind the counter.

"Now *who* did *this* to my fresh coconut cake?" Miss Nellie was pointing in frustration to what was once an elegant three-layer cake. The few kids who had gathered on barstools paused from licking their ice-cream cones and craned their necks to see the dessert. Marco and Maria joined Jake and Joy at the end of the counter for a look. It seemed as though someone had gnawed a big hunk out of the side of Miss Nellie's sweet specialty.

"And this isn't the only odd thing that's happened today," Miss Nellie said, throwing her hands up helplessly. "I'm missing a gallon—a gallon!—of milk and a bowl of homemade tuna salad from the refrigerator. Now I can be absent-minded sometimes, but this is ridiculous. I couldn't possibly have misplaced all that!"

Jake Bigsley peered over the top of his double-dip cone, fixed his large blue eyes on Marco and said, "This looks like a job for—"

"—*los dos amigos!*" Marco finished. Then he reached into his back pocket and pulled out a notebook and pen. "Miss Nellie," he said, "don't worry. Jake and I, here, we'll get to the bottom of this milk, cake, and tuna crime." Marco began to jot down some notes.

Jake nodded in agreement, his blond hair bouncing and swaying like wisps of wheat. "Marco and I will make sure that, once again, it will be safe for you to walk to your own refrigerator."

Marco caught a glimpse of Joy and Maria looking

up at the ceiling. He heard Maria whisper, "Oh, brother," and then Joy respond with, "You mean, oh, *brothers*."

Marco went over to Jake and put a firm grip on his friend's shoulder and squeezed. "Ignore them. This is just the sort of lack of respect we have to put up with to keep the streets safe for old women and young children."

Miss Nellie cleared her throat. "I certainly hope I don't fall into the category of being an old woman, Marco. I may be an old maid, but I'm not an old woman!"

Everyone laughed out loud. "No ma'am," Marco explained quickly. "You're not old at all! I mean, you're a grownup and all, but you're... I, uh, well... That was just a saying I heard on a TV detective show." Miss Nellie may not have married yet, but she was beautiful, inside and out, and everyone knew it. She was definitely not old. In fact, her strawberry blond curls made her look like a high-school girl when she let her hair down. But usually she piled up those wild pretty curls on top of her head. When she wore it that way, she reminded Marco of the women who wore high-neck lace collars in old-fashioned pictures he'd seen in books about the Wild West. Marco thought she was very pretty.

"Well," Miss Nellie said as she dusted off a barstool with her apron and sat down, "what can I do to help you gather clues?"

Marco tried to recover from his embarrassment. "I, uh… I'd like to ask you a few questions first," Marco explained. "I'll need to find out the names of everyone who has come into the store today, then I'd like to examine the evidence—the cake. Can we have permission to take it to our Secret Cabin Clubhouse to give it a good looking-over?"

"Sure," said Miss Nellie. "I sure can't sell it to customers now! I'll pack it up in a cardboard box, and then we'll get to those questions of yours."

Marco could hardly wait to get started, but he tried to hide his excitement. After all, this was serious business. Even so, he had to admit, there was nothing he and Jake Bigsley loved more than a good mystery.

Except maybe chocolate peanut-butter ice cream.

2

CAT BURGLAR?

J ake and Marco walked in the door of a small log cabin on the south side of Lake Willapango. This secluded area of Camp Wanna Banana wasn't far from the Garcia house, and the twins had discovered this old, abandoned house nearly a year ago. During summer camp, the cabin became the nature center with kids of all ages crawling all over the place. But Jake and Joy's dad, who owned the camp, allowed the Twiblings to use it as a Secret Cabin Clubhouse the rest of the year.

The cabin was only one room, but it had a little kitchen area with refrigerator, sink, table, and chairs, as well as a fireplace and an old sofa bed placed between two rocking chairs in the living area.

Marco placed the large cardboard box on the wooden table and carefully pulled out the cake with the plate attached.

"Got your flashlight?" Marco asked, looking expectantly at Jake.

"You bet," answered Jake, digging around in his emergency backpack. "Here you go."

Marco shone the light all around the cake and then held the beam steady in one place.

"See that?" he asked.

"What?" asked Jake.

"Those tiny little reddish hairs, about an inch long."

"Verrrry interesting," commented Jake, leaning in for a closer look.

"Whoever ate this cake had really short red hair," Marco said as he reached for his clue book and recorded the information.

"Marco, there's something else odd about this," Jake noted aloud.

"What?"

"Well, look at the teeth marks on the icing. The bite size is very tiny and the teeth holes are small— not much bigger than a thick needle would make."

"Yeah," said Marco, "good observation, amigo. And look at those long, smooth indentations around the edge of the frosting. Something with a small tongue licked this cake."

Marco added the information to the clue book, then looked up. "So what's your conclusion, Jake, based on the clues we have so far?"

"Well," said Jake, as he raised one eyebrow to indicate a flash of profound insight. "Looks to me like a tiny red-headed baby must have crawled up on the cabinet and started eating and licking Miss Nellie's cake while her back was turned. Then he must have crawled away on the floor and out the door."

Marco smiled. Jake tried hard, but he didn't always make sense. "Jake, I don't think a baby could climb up on the cabinet like that. Even if he could, I think Miss Nellie or the mother would have noticed. Babies aren't exactly the quietest things."

"Then who do *you* think it was, Mr. Genius Scientist?" Jake asked, sounding slightly offended.

Marco thought for a minute.

"Hey, Mr. Henley came by Miss Nellie's today, remember?"

"Yeah," said Jake. "But he doesn't have red hair or little tiny teeth or a little bitty mouth."

"Noooo," said Marco, "but Pumpkin does!"

"That's right!" said Jake. "Pumpkin must have helped herself to a hunk of coconut cake while Miss Nellie and Mr. Henley were visiting. Mystery solved!"

"Not so fast," answered Marco. "As smart as Pumpkin might be, and as much as she loves milk and tuna, I don't think she could have opened the fridge and hauled off a gallon of milk and a bowl of tuna salad. Unnoticed."

"Hmmm," Jake agreed. "Sounds like we've got some more detective work to do."

"Let's go back to Miss Nellie's tomorrow after school and ask her some more questions. We just don't have enough clues to go on yet."

Jake nodded. Then after a short period of silence he said, "Marco?"

"What Jake?"

"Do you think this cake is completely *covered* in cat germs?"

Marco knew that his friend loved sweet treats, and the smell of the coconut frosting was tempting both of their hungry tummies.

"Better not eat the evidence, buddy, " Marco said, lightly slapping Jake's back. "Let's put the cake in the freezer and then head to my house. Mama's making sopaipillas!"

"Those little puffy bread things you fill up with honey and butter?" Jake asked hopefully.

"*Sí,* señor," Marco replied.

And with that, they set off in search of a snack. The mystery would have to remain unsolved until tomorrow.

3

NOT THE USUAL SUSPECTS

The next day, after school, Jamie Klem invited Maria and Joy to go with her family to the library. The Klems' giant, old avocado-green station wagon was just big enough to carry everyone.

After waving good-bye to their sisters, Jake and Marco headed straight to Miss Nellie's Café. They had exactly twenty minutes before Mr. Bigsley would be there to take them home.

"Hey, Jake," Marco asked, "do you ever wish you were rich?"

"Oh yeah," Jake answered. "You mean rich like Chad Riggs must be?"

Marco nodded. "I love my parents, but we never have enough money to buy the really cool stuff—the cool jeans, new bikes, you know. The good stuff. Name-brand stuff."

"I know," Jake agreed. "Our dads didn't exactly pick the world's best-paying jobs when they decided to run a camp for kids. Dad's doing some carpentry work over in Whispering Pines Estates on some of those big new houses, and Mom gives piano lessons on Saturdays now to help pay some of our bills."

"Yeah, my dad's shoeing horses, and Mama is selling her homemade tamales to the Tall Pines Deli," Marco sympathized. "Do you ever wish your dad would get a job that pays more, with a suit and a big paycheck and everything?"

"Sometimes," Jake answered. "But our dads love us, and they do things with us—like riding horses and playing ball and just hanging out and talking. I just think maybe I'm rich in other ways."

"Maaaybe," said Marco. "But I can't wait until I grow up and can start making some real money. There's no way I'm going to settle for being as poor as my dad is."

Jake and Marco rounded the corner near Miss Nellie's, then stopped and stared at the café display window. Jake let out a low whistle. Everything that had been there yesterday was gone—the bales of hay, the rocking chair, and the quilts.

"What happened to your country window decorations?" Marco asked Miss Nellie as the two boys walked through the door and up to the counter. Miss Nellie brushed a stray curl off her forehead and tucked it back in place.

"You are not going to believe this, boys, but when I got here this morning everything was gone. I'm also missing a big tub of peanut butter and a loaf of bread from the pantry. Not to mention about fifteen dollars in quarters from the cookie jar where I save change from the soda machine."

"Now that's odd," said Marco, scratching his head.

"Did you get a chance to examine the cake?" Miss Nellie asked, leaning across the counter with a smile.

"Yes," said Marco. "The evidence points to Mr. Henley's cat."

Miss Nellie blushed. "Oh, that's right! Pumpkin loves sweets and breads! Mr. Henley and I were… uh…so busy visiting that I guess I didn't notice the cat." There was something about the way Miss Nellie said the words "Mr. Henley and I" that made Marco curious.

"Are you and Mr. Henley becoming really good friends?" Marco asked.

Miss Nellie chuckled. "Well, you may as well know, young man, that yesterday he asked me to marry him!" Miss Nellie had often talked about wanting to have a big family of her own someday. The way she obviously enjoyed kids, Marco was sure she would get married someday, but he dreaded the embarrassing, lovey-dovey looks that would surely be on Mr. Henley's and Miss Nellie's faces from now on. He didn't know what to say.

Jake had a grimace on his face. "What's the matter, Jake?" Miss Nellie asked. "Don't you like romance and love and weddings?"

Marco and Jake laughed and made gagging motions at the same time.

The café door opened and Mr. Henley poked his head in, wiggling a big metal key ring. Mr. Henley had let Marco examine the ring last fall, and Marco knew each key was attached to a label, including one that said "hardware store," another "Nellie's," and another "art shop." It was Mr. Henley's duty to unlock and lock up their section of the town square. "Nellie, you'd better let me change your locks before you head home tonight. I've had several boards of lumber, some nails, a hammer, and a saw stolen from my shop sometime during the night, along with a small microwave oven I kept in the shop kitchen."

Miss Nellie looked frightened. "Ken, what's happening?"

"I don't know, hon, I don't know."

Marco carefully recorded Mr. Henley's missing items in his clue book. How did all the stolen items fit together? He tapped his pencil on the paper in an effort to sort out the clues.

What came to mind was…absolutely nothing.

That night at supper, Marco was quiet, still trying to figure out what could be happening in town.

Maria, however, was extra talkative. "Oh, Mama! Joy and I had *so* much fun at the library with Jamie's family today. Thanks for letting me go. They are so funny, and there are so many of them! It's like being in the middle of a circus with crazy stuff going on everywhere you turn. Toddlers laughing, sisters chatting nonstop in Southern accents, brothers playing tricks on each other. Their old car is about to come apart at the seams. In fact, after we went to the library, we had to stop by their house to put some water in the radiator so we could make it to Camp Wanna Banana. But the whole family seems to be having too much fun to worry about things falling apart around them."

Mama laughed and then asked, "What does their house look like, Maria?"

"It's kind of like their car—big and old but lots of fun. In fact, their dad had a bunch of lumber stacked up in the yard and was building a front porch."

Marco sat up, suddenly very attentive. "Was the lumber from Henley's store?" Marco asked.

Maria thought a minute, "You know, come to think of it, the wood was wrapped in a big plastic thing with Henley's Hardware stamped on it. But why do you ask?"

"I'm just wondering," Marco replied. "That's all. Just wondering."

Marco walked upstairs after dinner to his attic room across the hall from Maria's. His room was so small that it barely held a bed and a small desk. He had to keep his clothes in drawers underneath the bed, and this, for some reason, had really begun to bother him. "This is ridiculous!" he found himself shouting in frustration. "I need a bigger room!"

Maria heard Marco's outburst and poked her head in his room. "What's the matter with you lately, Marco? It never used to bother you that we live in a small house and don't have much money. In fact, you never cared about your clothes or how you looked at all! You and Jake would wear just about anything you found in the laundry room, no matter how crazy it looked. But lately you just seem to have a bad case of 'the wants.' "

"I know, I know," Marco had to agree. Maybe he was growing out of some of his little-kid ways. Or maybe it was something else gnawing at his heart. Something his Sunday-school teacher called greed.

Maria shook her head and said softly, "Maybe you ought to pray about being more thankful for what we do have, Marco. This just isn't like you. You've always been the brother I could depend on to remind *me* to trust God to give us whatever we need."

Marco couldn't answer his sister because he knew

she was right, and yet he could not change the way he felt. Maybe God could change his feelings. He would pray about that before he went to sleep tonight. Right now, though, he wanted to write something down in his clue book.

He went to his backpack, grabbed his notebook and pencil, and sat down on the floor. He wrote *Suspects* and then underlined the word. Underneath *Suspects,* he wrote *Mr. Klem.* After all, Jamie's father must be under a lot of pressure to feed all those kids, and they obviously didn't have much money. Maybe he stole the milk and tuna to feed his family. *And what about the lumber for a front porch?* Marco thought to himself, leaning back against the bed. *Is it just a coincidence that the lumber is from Mr. Henley's store? Looks like Jamie's father also has a bad case of "the wants,"* Marco mused. *Only he decided to steal what he wanted. At least I haven't stooped that low!*

But if Mr. Klem was stealing from Miss Nellie and Mr. Henley, how was he doing it? Only Mr. Henley and Miss Nellie had keys to their stores, Marco remembered. Then he sat up with a start. *Mr. Henley! It could have been Mr. Henley who stole the items from Miss Nellie's Café!* Immediately, Marco argued with himself. *But Mr. Henley loves Miss Nellie. And why would he need stuff like milk and tuna anyway?*

Still, a good detective never overlooked any suspect until the crime was solved. And Mr. Henley did have the only other key to Miss Nellie's store. With that, Marco sadly penciled Ken Henley underneath Mr. Klem's name on his growing list of suspects.

4

PEANUT-BUTTER CLUES

The next day at school, Marco shared his thoughts with his partner in crime solving.

"Man, oh man," Jake said as the boys stood in front of their lockers, which were next to each other. "Either way, somebody's gonna be hurt. Think of poor Jamie's family. What if her father is a thief? What if he gets sent to jail? And Miss Nellie! She was so happy about marrying Mr. Henley, but if he's stealing from her... Hey, wait a minute, Marco. It couldn't have been Mr. Henley!"

"Why not?" Marco asked as he shoved his history

book into the locker and shut the metal door. "Because Mr. Henley was also the victim of a crime. Remember, he had lumber and stuff stolen from his shop yesterday too."

"I thought of that," Marco said. "But all we really know is that Mr. Henley *said* he was robbed. Maybe he just pretended to have been robbed in order throw us off his trail!"

"I dunno," said Jake. "That seems pretty unlikely to me."

"Still," Marco said as he and Jake walked toward the school cafeteria. "We have to keep him on the list of suspects until we have more proof."

Jake nodded. "Did Miss Nellie or Mr. Henley call the police about this yet?"

"I'm not sure," Marco answered. "Let's ask them this afternoon. Right now, let's get to the lunchroom. I'm starving!"

"Me too," said Jake rubbing his flat tummy. "It's chili-dog and macaroni-and-cheese day!"

"Anybody wanna trade?" a girl's voice, thick with a Southern accent, drawled. "I hate peanut buttuh and jelly."

Chad Riggs, who was sitting across from Jamie, shook his head no as he glanced inside his new neon orange lunchbox with a picture on the lid of Kobe Bryant doing a slam dunk. "Sorry, Jamie, all I've got is peanut butter too."

Jamie frowned. "That's okay. Hey, Chad, I saw you workin' at Miss Nellie's the othuh day. How come a rich kid like you is workin'?"

Chad laughed. "Well, my dad's got a good paying job right now—he's a traveling salesman—but he grew up poor, and so he makes me work for half of most things I want. Says it's good for me. Last summer I mowed lawns in the town where we lived to earn money for basketball shoes and video games and stuff."

Marco felt a pang of guilt. He assumed that all Chad had to do was ask for things he wanted and his parents shelled out the money.

Joy Bigsley reached in her lunch kit and pulled out a Baggie with a sandwich inside. "I'll trade you my ham sandwich, Jamie."

Jamie nodded and reached over the lunch table to complete the trade. "Thaaank you, Joah. I'm so sick of peanut buttuh I think could faint on the lunch table right this minute if I have to look at it again. It's all we've had lately!"

Marco's detective ears perked up at this news from across the school lunchroom table. "Really, Jamie?"

"Yessireee! It's like my mothuh's turned into a peanut brain ever since Daddy brought home this huge plastic bucket of peanut buttuh. Yesterday aftahnoon it was peanut-buttuh cookies. This mornin' she made peanut-buttuh pancakes. Last night she fed us these noodles with peanut-buttuh sauce, some dish from a fahaway country called Thailand. She found it in her *Cookin' from Around the World* cookbook."

"Yeah," echoed one of Jamie's little brothers from down the table a ways. "She called it Pad Thai Oriental noodles. But it was nothin' but spaghetti with peanut buttuh and a bunch of ol' vegetables on top!"

A long, loud "Eeeewww!" went from kid to kid down the length of the lunch table as everyone but Marco made a different disgusted face. Marco was busy quietly jotting a note in his clue book. Under the word *Evidence,* he quickly jotted *Large pail of peanut butter at the Klems' house. Same as missing peanut butter from Miss Nellie's Café?*

Then he cleared his throat and asked, "Jamie, where'd your father get such a big bucket of peanut butter anyway? They don't sell those huge containers at Tall Pines Grocery, do they?"

"Naw," said Jamie. "He brought it home yestahday from one of those big discount warehouse stores in Desert City. He went aftah he picked up lumbuh for the porch from Mr. Henleh."

Marco nodded sadly. He hated to think how Jamie would feel when she found out her father had stolen both the peanut butter and the lumber. Mr. Klem just moved up to his number-one suspect.

"What kind of sandwich did you have yesterday?" Marco asked, secretly checking for another clue.

"Tuna-fish salad," Jamie answered with a smile. "My favorite."

Jake looked over at Marco and raised one eyebrow. He, too, was catching on. Marco gave a small nod of understanding. Miss Nellie's missing tuna salad must have ended up in Jamie's lunch as well.

Marco only wished he could keep Jamie as clueless as she was right now.

5

RUNAWAYS

After school, Marco and Maria, along with Jake and Joy, headed over to Miss Nellie's to wait for Mrs. Bigsley to pick them up.

Maria stopped suddenly and nodded toward a thin, brown-haired girl walking across the town square. She looked to be about thirteen or fourteen and was holding hands with a preschooler who was maybe three years old. They were walking toward Henley's Hardware. "Who are they?" Maria asked.

"I don't know," Joy answered. "I've never seen them before. Maybe they're new."

The girl stopped near Mr. Henley's store and looked around as if to see whether anyone noticed them. Then she pulled the smaller girl around the side of the store, and the two were out of sight.

"What are they doing?" Marco asked.

"I don't know," Jake said. "But let's follow them and find out."

The Twiblings followed the steps of the two girls around the corner, behind the hardware store, but the pair had disappeared.

Scratching his head, Marco commented, "Now that's weird. Where could they have gone so quickly?"

The other three friends shook their heads, looking equally puzzled.

"Must have run off into the woods back here," Jake said. "Maybe they're taking a shortcut home through the trees or something."

"We'd better get back to Miss Nellie's!" Maria interrupted. "Your mom will be here to pick us up soon."

"Afternoon, Miss Nellie!" Marco called as he opened the door to the café and walked in for a quick visit. "Anything else missing today?"

"As a matter of fact," Miss Nellie said as she leaned her arms on the counter, "today I am missing a little doll I used to keep up on the shelf for decoration—a doll I was given when I was just a little girl. But other than that, everything seems to be in place. It's a real puzzle to me, guys. These thieves pick the oddest things to take. After the quarters were missing, I've been careful not to leave any money lying around, so you'd think they'd steal from somebody else who had things of more value."

"Did you call the police?" Jake asked.

"At first it seemed silly to call the police. I mean, how do you report a case of missing tuna and a jug of milk? But after Mr. Henley got robbed and more things disappeared here, we did report it to the police late yesterday afternoon."

"What did they say?" Marco asked.

"They said they'd keep an eye out, but, of course, I told them I also had the Dos Amigos Detectives on the case as well," she said with a wink. "Any suspects yet, boys?"

Marco nodded. "Yes, but I'm not pointing any fingers until I have more evidence. It's against our Dos Amigos Detectives Code of Honor. We're getting closer to the truth, but there are still too many questions and not enough answers."

"Miss Nellie," Jake interrupted, as if a thought suddenly occurred to him, "have you seen a couple of new girls in town? An older one with a younger one?"

"Funny you should ask that, Jake," Nellie answered. "The other day at the library I saw a girl— maybe about junior-high age—holding a young child in her lap, reading her a Dr. Seuss book. It was the middle of the school day, so I thought it was odd that they weren't in school. But then, there are lots of homeschooling families these days, and they spend a lot of time at the library." Miss Nellie paused a moment, then added, "Since Whispering Pines Estates opened up, our little town is beginning to grow. I actually see people at the grocery store these days that I've never met before! So I guess it's not all that unusual to see a couple of new kids walking around town. We'd better get used to it, kids!"

A horn honked outside. It was Mrs. Bigsley driving up in her red minivan. She was wearing overalls and a giant pink sun hat. Even from inside the store, Marco could see her singing a happy tune to herself, as Munch-Munch, Joy's pet spider monkey, danced up and down in the front seat. Since Mrs. Bigsley had given the two sets of twins their Twiblings nickname, Marco and Maria had decided to give Mrs. Bigsley one of her own: Merry Sunshine. She was nearly always cheerful, even if she was a little scatterbrained sometimes.

"Gotta go!" Joy said to Miss Nellie before turning to leave.

Miss Nellie nodded, then called out after the kids, "Tell your mom I said hello, Joy. And tell her I need to talk to her about playing the piano for our wedding!"

"Hi, Mrs. Bigsley," Marco said cheerfully as he climbed in the van behind Joy and Maria and Jake. "Nice hat you got there." Munch-Munch jumped up and down, her yellow polka-dot ruffled skirt bouncing as she demanded some attention. Marco reached out to pet her head. "And very nice dress you have on there, too, Munchy."

"Why, thank you, Marco," Mrs. Bigsley said, reaching for an enormous pair of purple sunglasses and propping them on her nose. "And Munchy thanks you too."

With this, the monkey reached in Mrs. Bigsley's bag for her own miniature pair of pink sunshades, put them on, and settled back against the car seat with a tired sigh.

Everyone laughed.

"So, how are my Twiblings today?" Mrs. Bigsley asked.

"We're fine," Jake answered. "Just peachy."

Mrs. Bigsley smiled and nodded, then lowered her sunglasses and adjusted the radio knob, searching for her favorite station. As she turned the dial, a news announcer said something about "missing children," and Mrs. Bigsley paused to listen to the rest of the story.

The announcer's deep voice continued. "The missing children—two girls and one boy, all siblings— were put in three separate Desert City foster homes after their parents were killed in a car accident this past winter. Investigators believe the children managed to find each other and are on the run, possibly in hiding. A picture of the missing siblings will appear in local and surrounding newspapers tomorrow."

"Why did they run away?" Jake asked.

Marco shot a look at Jake and asked, "How would you feel if somebody wanted to separate you and Joy, especially if you'd already lost your parents?"

Jake looked over at Joy and seemed sad just thinking about it. Marco and Maria exchanged sympathetic glances as well. As twin siblings, they all had their share of brother-sister fights and arguments. But they loved each other something fierce as well.

"If someone tried to separate me from Marco," Maria said with great feeling, "I think I'd try to find him too!"

Marco beamed at his sister, feeling a nice warmth spreading inside him, like a good cup of hot chocolate. Then, as if someone had pulled an invisible puppet string on the top of his head, Marco said, "The two girls we saw today! Could they be the runaways?"

Jake nodded. "Maybe, but the report said there was a boy with them too."

"Hmmm," said Marco. "You could be right. But I think we ought to investigate all the same."

6

PUTTING FOUR HEADS TOGETHER

Marco called an emergency meeting at the Secret Cabin Clubhouse that afternoon. He and Jake had decided to include their sisters this time, since so many mysteries were piling up one on top of another. He figured it wouldn't hurt to have all the thinking power they could get, even if it would have to come from girls' brains.

Marco and Maria arrived first and leaned their bicycles against the clubhouse. Marco saw Jake and Joy paddling their canoe across the lake toward shore.

Munch-Munch had two skinny arms wrapped around Joy's neck.

Within minutes the friends had plopped down on the braided rug in front of the fireplace. Munchy hopped on the sofa bed and then busied herself with taking things out of Jake's backpack and putting them in her mouth. Marco tried to ignore the funny pet, but it wasn't easy. This cute little monkey whom everyone loved inspired Camp Wanna Banana's name. Whenever Munchy was around, chaos was usually nearby.

Marco cleared his throat. Munch-Munch stuck a flashlight in her mouth and turned it on. Her little face lit up from inside like a hairy lantern. "No, Munchy!" said Joy as she took the flashlight away and ordered the monkey to sit still in her lap.

Marco cleared his throat again, trying to get on to the serious matters at hand.

"Did your mom call the sheriff about the girls we saw today?" he asked Joy.

"Yes," she said. "She told them we'd seen two girls about the same age as two of the missing kids, and that they're probably somewhere in the woods behind the shops downtown. By the time we got home, it was nearly dark, and Mom said they would probably send out a search party in the morning to check out our information."

"If these are the runaway sisters, I wonder where the missing boy is?" asked Maria.

Marco nodded. "I know. I've wondered that, too. But until we see the picture tomorrow, we won't even know if the girls we saw today are the runaways. We may be making a big deal out of nothing."

Jake scratched his head. "Do you think it's possible that the missing kids have something to do with the missing stuff?"

Marco smiled and took out his detective pad. "I've been wondering the same thing. If the kids are runaways, they would be looking for food—like milk, peanut butter, and tuna fish."

"And maybe they stole the lumber to make a shelter in the woods!" Joy suggested.

"Possibly." Marco nodded his head as he jotted down more notes.

"But what would they do with a microwave oven in the woods?" Maria asked curiously.

Marco looked at his sister and gave her a proud smile. "That's using your head, Maria. What *would* they do with a microwave when there is no electricity in the woods?"

"Maybe they used it for a cabinet or a stool to sit on or something," Jake offered.

"Hmmm," Marco mused. "I suppose that could be true."

Maria's eyes widened. "Miss Nellie's missing doll!" she said. "Maybe the kids stole the doll for the little sister to play with."

"Could be," agreed Joy, her eyes lighting up with the connection. Munch-Munch looked up at her and patted Joy's cheek, as if approving of Joy's every word.

Marco scribbled all the possibilities into his notebook. Munch-Munch, having sat still as long as she could, now leaped out of Joy's lap and over to Marco, grabbing his pen and running out the door, squealing with glee. If a monkey could talk, Marco knew she'd be saying, "Come chase me!"

He stood up, shook his head, and darted out the door after one naughty monkey and his favorite pen.

7

HOT OFF THE PRESS

The next morning at school, Marco and Maria walked toward their lockers and heard the noisy roar of kids talking excitedly.

"What's going on?" Marco wondered aloud.

"I don't know," answered Maria. "Let's check it out."

"Sounds like all the noise is coming from Mr. Fields's science room," said Marco, glancing down the hall. "Come on!"

The twins nearly ran into Jake and Joy as they scurried into Mr. Fields's room to investigate.

Several students and a few teachers were gathered around Mr. Fields's desk. Marco pushed his way to the center of the talking crowd and saw that everyone was looking at the morning issue of the *Pine Tree Gazette*.

There, on the front page, was a picture of the runaway orphans. The two girls looked exactly like the girls the twins had spied downtown yesterday. But the greatest shock was the picture of the runaway brother.

It was none other than Chad Riggs.

Mr. Fields picked up the paper and read it aloud.

The missing children are named Michael, Melissa, and Misty Parsons, but they may be calling themselves by other names to disguise their identities. They were last seen two weeks ago. Since they are believed to have less than $75, they are probably not more than 100 miles from where they were last seen in Desert City. Police are following a tip about the possibility of the children being in the Tall Pines area today.

Mr. Fields looked up from the paper and sat down, calling the class to order. "Everyone have a seat, please." The children's roar finally calmed to a low murmur and then silence. Every eye was on Mr. Fields.

"Kids," Mr. Fields said, "has anyone seen Chad this morning?"

All heads in the class turned back and forth, silently answering no.

"How about last night?"

Again, no one had seen the new student since school let out yesterday afternoon.

Mr. Fields cleared his throat. "Has anyone here ever been to Chad's house? Know where he lives? Met anyone he is staying with?"

Finally, Jamie Klem raised her hand. "Chad always rode his bike toward Whisperin' Pines aftah school. I once asked him which house he lived in, but he just kinda avoided my question."

"Thank you, Jamie," Mr. Fields answered. "Obviously Chad has been through more pain and hurt than any of us in this class realized. He probably saw the morning paper and has left with his sisters. They may not even be in town now."

Marco raised his hand. "Mr. Fields, would it be okay for us to pray for him and his sisters?"

Mr. Fields nodded. "Marco, I think if there were ever a time for prayer in school, this would be it. I know all of you kids in this classroom. Lots of you come to my nature center at Camp Wanna Banana, and many of you are in my Sunday-school class. Let's close our eyes and, if you'd like to, take a moment to pray for Chad—actually, I guess we need to start calling him by his real name, Michael."

Everyone in class bowed their heads silently for several minutes. Marco thought how lost and frightened Michael must feel. He prayed two prayers. In the first Marco asked God to protect Michael and his sisters and to find a way to help them all stay together. In the second he asked God to forgive him for not realizing sooner that being rich has nothing to do with fancy tennis shoes, bicycles, or big houses. Being rich is all about being wanted and loved.

And Marco knew he was most definitely rich.

8

MARCO'S BIG IDEA

The phone rang almost as soon as Marco and Maria walked in the door after school. It was Jake's voice coming through the receiver.

"Meet us at the clubhouse?"

"Be there in fifteen minutes," Marco answered, gesturing to Maria to hurry and get ready. Then he paused before adding, "Hey, Jake? Why don't you suggest that Joy leave Munch-Munch at home today? We've got serious business to discuss, and, well, you know how Munchy can be." Jake agreed and Marco turned to get ready to leave.

Before long the foursome was gathered at the cabin. It was warm today, so they sat on the front porch, enjoying the sun and the spring wildflowers splattered like bright paint spills in the wild grass around them.

Marco spoke first, having already begun processing his thoughts about the clues. "Chad—I mean *Michael*—and his sisters have moved to being number-one suspects in the café and hardware burglary case. Do you agree?"

"I'm not sure," Joy asked. "Why do you suspect them as the thieves?"

"Well, they have a motive. They are homeless and hungry."

Jake raised his eyebrows. "How do you know that? Maybe they're staying with someone who is hiding them."

"Maybe," Marco agreed.

"I'd say Mr. Klem is still a suspect," Jake insisted. "He has a pretty good motive too."

"I just can't believe that," Joy whispered with a sigh.

Maria scratched her head. "Why do you think Michael went to school and not the sisters?"

"I think they probably all wanted to go to school," Joy ventured, "but they were afraid of being found out if the three of them walked into school together. The oldest, Melissa, must have decided to take care of the little sister, Misty, during the day."

Jake spoke next. "Maybe Michael had to go to school in order to be able to work in the town, mowing lawns or doing odd jobs. If he didn't go to school, at his age, some adult would have reported him to authorities."

"Man," Marco confessed. "I have been so jealous of Ch—*Michael*, I mean. It seemed like everything he owned was brand-new!"

"It was," said Jake. "Brand-new and mostly freshly stolen, so it now appears."

"I wonder how they got from Desert City to Tall Pines?" Maria asked.

"Seventy-five dollars would have gotten them bus tickets here," Joy answered. "And they may have shoplifted clothes and food from that shopping center just south of Tall Pines. I heard that a couple of teenagers who went shopping there didn't lock up their new bikes and had them stolen."

"Where do you think they're hiding now?" Jake

asked, leaning back against a porch post and nearly slipping off of it in the process.

"They might not be far," Marco said. "I'd guess they've run out of money by now, and they can only get around on foot or a bike. They would still need money and food, and somehow they've been able to get in and out of Henley's Hardware and Miss Nellie's without being noticed—" Marco stopped in mid-sentence and looked as though he'd been struck by idea lightning.

"What?" Jake asked excitedly. "What is it?"

"I think I may know where they are," Marco said. "Let's ask Mama to take us over to Miss Nellie's early in the morning, before school. There's something I want to check out."

"Marco," said Maria sadly, "I almost don't want to find them. I'd hate for those kids to have to go back to foster homes. And what if the police take their little sister away from the older kids? She looked so cute and trusting of her big sister the other day."

"I know, Maria, I know," said Marco. "But it's better that we find them first. Maybe we can find a way to help them before the police move in."

9

BACK-ROOM INVESTIGATION

"Good morning, Miss Nellie!" the four friends said as they pushed open the door.

"Well, hey, kiddos," Nellie said as she smiled in greeting and surprise. "What are you all doing in the café so early this morning?"

"Marco thinks he may have figured out the mystery," Jake said.

"Oh, really?" Miss Nellie said as she leaned on the counter, curious. "Tell me what you've got."

Marco loved the way Miss Nellie always treated

him—as if he were a real detective. She never looked down on him or Jake or made fun of them the way Joy and Maria sometimes did.

Pulling out his notebook, he said, "Miss Nellie, you know about the runaway kids—and you know one of them was pretending to be Chad Riggs, right?"

"Yes," Nellie said, "I do. You know, Marco, there was something about that Chad kid that I really liked. He was a hard worker, and he seemed a little bit of a loner, but I could always get him to talk. Funny, he always ordered a triple dip of ice cream— one dip on the cone, two dips in a cup. I thought he was just a big eater. Now I realize he was taking ice cream to his sisters!"

"What kind of work did he do for you?" Marco asked.

"Oh, dipping ice cream, cleaning up tables, sweeping out the back room…"

"Could I see that back room please?" Marco interrupted.

"Sure," Nellie said, her eyes questioning, appearing eager to discover what was on Marco's mind. "Come on back."

The four friends followed Nellie around to the back of the store, where she kept her cooking supplies and the big industrial refrigerator. Marco surveyed the wall facing the vacated art studio next door. "Can I look behind that big ice-cream poster leaning against the wall?"

"Sure," Nellie said. "I keep meaning to clean this mess out. But you know how that goes."

Marco lifted the poster of brightly colored ice-cream flavors from its position on the floor. Miss Nellie and the girls gasped.

10

HIDEAWAY HOME

Behind the poster, a gaping hole big enough for a person to crawl through had been jaggedly cut out of the wall.

"Come on," Marco said to his friend. "Let's see what's on the other side."

Jake crawled through first. A few moments later Marco heard him saying, "You've gotta see this. You won't believe it."

Marco crawled through next, then stood in awe at his surroundings.

Someone had transformed Andy's Art Studio into a little makeshift home.

In a corner under some watercolor paintings, near a stack of library books on the floor nearby, was the rocking chair from the window display. Someone had built three sets of bed frames from freshly cut lumber and placed hay and quilts atop them as mattresses. A roughly cut kitchen table and a shelf stood in another corner. On the table was Mr. Henley's missing microwave oven and a tan-colored plastic bucket that had once been full of peanut butter.

Jake picked up a small stack of papers from the shelf. "Look at this, Marco. School enrollment forms with Chad's name on them."

Marco examined them closely. "Michael changed his name and forged parents' signatures on this one," he said. "Look here." Jake leaned over Marco's shoulder for a closer look. "He used Wite-Out on this medical form and papers from past schools to erase the names. Then he must have copied them at the school library to make them look like originals."

Jake nodded. "Now I remember overhearing the principal ask Michael about his parents that first week he came to school. He told her that his dad was traveling with his sales job, and his mom had to go stay with his sick grandmother, so they couldn't enroll him in person. He said he'd have his aunt, who was watching him for the week, fax the forms."

"One thing is for sure," Marco admitted. "Chad—er, Michael I mean, is no dummy."

"There's my quilt!" Miss Nellie said as she crawled through and stood up beside Marco and Jake. "And Ken's microwave! And the peanut butter…" Her voice trailed off as she stood and stared in silent surprise.

Soon Maria and Joy were inside the gallery-turned-runaways'-home.

"Those poor kids," said Maria.

"I know," said Joy. "They did the best they could, didn't they?"

"Yes," said Maria. "Hey, look over here, behind the bed. There's another hole. I'll bet that leads to the hardware store."

Jake walked over to where Maria was standing and peered through the wall. "What a perfect hiding place. They could steal food from Miss Nellie's and lumber and hardware from Mr. Henley's and never have to break through any front doors."

"And here must be where they got into the building in the first place," said Marco, pointing to a stepstool and an unlocked window at the back of the empty store, facing the alley. He stood on tiptoe and looked out.

Marco found that he was feeling a jumble of emotions. He hated that anyone would lie to him and his friends or steal from a nice lady like Miss Nellie. But then Marco had never been through the sort of hard times and hurt that Michael and his sisters had gone through. Marco didn't know what it felt like to be that desperate.

"Where do you think they are now?" asked Jake.

Marco surveyed the surroundings. No bicycles, no clothes. He wondered how far the sisters and their brother could have gone since the night before.

"I have no idea," he said.

Marco heard the sad low sound of sniffling and looked toward the source of the crying. To his surprise, it was Miss Nellie. She had found the old rag doll on the rocking chair and was now sitting in the chair, holding the doll in her lap. Silent tears ran down her cheeks.

"What's wrong, Miss Nellie?" Maria asked. She

walked over to their friend and patted her shoulder. "What's the matter?"

"Oh, Maria," Miss Nellie answered softly. "I was once a little girl without parents too. It was a very long time ago."

"Can you tell us about it?" Joy asked. Marco and Jake sat down quietly on the edge of the hay-covered beds.

"Well," she said between sniffs, "I was about five years old when my father left me and my mother alone. Then my mother drove me to my grandmother's house one day, kissed me good-bye, and never re-turned. I thought my little heart would break."

Marco imagined Miss Nellie as a young child, abandoned by her parents. No wonder she wanted a big family of her own so much! She wanted to love other children in ways she'd never been loved by her own parents.

Miss Nellie hugged the ragged doll to her chest. "My grandmother dried my tears and took me to her sewing room and told me, 'Honey, we're going to make you something special. Something you can love and hang on to forever.' She took bits of material and yarn and thread and made me this little rag doll."

Miss Nellie lifted the doll's dress. "See, this is where Granny embroidered a heart. She said that she put all her love in this heart, and that if I ever needed a little of her love and she wasn't around, I could hug my rag doll and remember I would always, always be loved by Granny."

Suddenly, Miss Nellie sat up as if an angel had brushed by her face, giving her clear directions from heaven. "Children," she said, "go get Mr. Henley. There's something I want to ask him. Then we need to start praying and searching for those precious kids."

11

INTRUDERS!

It had been a long day. Marco and his friends were late to school after showing the hideout in Andy's Art Studio to Mr. Henley.

Miss Nellie and Mr. Henley had assured the four friends that everything would be all right. They were optimistic that when the missing children were found, God would make a way for the brother and sisters to stay together.

"Come by after school," Miss Nellie had told them. "I'll have a surprise waiting for you."

When the Twiblings arrived at the shop, Miss

Nellie handed them a big box. "I made this for you to thank you for helping me! Maybe the four of you can share it when you meet at your clubhouse!"

Marco opened the box and laughed out loud. Inside was one of Nellie's famous coconut cakes, shaped like a cat's face—with pointy ears, black licorice whiskers, and orange-dyed coconut sprinkles all over it. Miss Nellie laughed and then said, "I call it Miss Pumpkin's Surprise."

Now Marco carried the box up the path to the cabin, shifting the weight of his backpack to his other shoulder, Maria following close behind him. Maria had often teased him and Jake for always carrying their backpacks with them in the woods—until this past winter when Marco and Maria had been carried away on a runaway horse and had to spend the night in the woods. They had survived on his healthy nutty snacks and powdered cocoa mix. And she had never teased him again about his backpack.

"Jake and Joy must have beat us here!" Marco said. "The lights are already on in the window, and I can hear them talking."

But as they approached the cabin, Maria stopped suddenly and whispered, "Marco, look!"

There, partially hidden by the low branches of a tree, were two shiny mountain bikes. One was bright blue, and the other one, neon yellow, had a child's bicycle seat strapped to the back of it.

"They're here!" Marco whispered loudly. "What now?"

"I don't know," Maria whispered back. "You're the brilliant detective with all the answers."

"Okay," said Marco. "Let's just go up to the door and knock."

Together the twins walked to the door of the cabin. As Marco raised his fist to knock, a familiar boy's voice said, "I'm going down by the lake," and suddenly, they were face to face with their runaway friend. Michael shouted out in surprise but recovered quickly.

"It's okay!" Michael said to his sisters, who were now stiff with fright. "It's Marco and Maria Garcia. I know them from school."

"Are you okay?" Marco asked.

"We're fine," said Michael defensively. "At least we were fine. How did you find us here?"

"This is our cabin. It's part of Camp Wanna Banana where we live and our parents work."

An invisible weight pressed down on Michael's shoulders, making them droop with discouragement. "Oh," he said sadly. "We thought we'd found a safe place to hide for the night. We were planning to move on in the morning." Maria walked around the boys and held out her hand to the oldest girl.

"Hi," she said, "I'm Maria. And you're Melissa, right?"

The girl nodded. Maria bent down to look at the young child, whose enormous blue eyes were staring up in fear. "It's okay, little one," said Maria. "You must be Misty. I'm not going to hurt you. We want to help you."

The girl clung tightly to her sister until Maria said, "Guess what we have for you?"

Marco walked over beside Maria, set his backpack on the table, then opened the box. He bent over to show Misty the coconut kitty-cat cake.

The adorable child smiled, revealing charming dimples. Rubbing her tiny tummy, she said, "I yike kitty-cat cake. I yike it a *yot!*" She jumped off her sister's lap to reach for the cake.

Then suddenly, to Marco's shock, the little girl closed her eyes and crumpled into a heap on the floor.

12

BACK TO LIFE

Marco dropped the cake in his hurry to pick up little Misty. He set her gently on the sleeper sofa and tried to remember everything he'd read in his Red Cross handbook. First he checked her vital signs. She was breathing. Pulse, good. He gently lifted her eyelids. Eyes normal, though rolled slightly back in her head.

By this time, Michael and Melissa were on their knees beside their sister, filled with panic.

Marco looked up and said, "Maria, wet a rag with

cool water. Michael, prop her feet up with one of those cushions."

Both obeyed without question. Maria grabbed a kitchen towel from the rough kitchen cabinet and pumped cold water onto the rag, wringing out the excess.

"Here, Marco," she said in worried tones as she handed her brother the damp rag.

Marco gently placed the cool rag across Misty's head. The child's eyelashes started to flutter softly like moth wings.

"Misty!" Melissa said, reaching for her little sister's hand. "Wake up, baby girl. Are you okay? Talk to us!"

Slowly, Misty opened her eyes. Sighs of relief went from one person to another as they stood, sat, and knelt around the tiny figure on the bed.

"Where kitty-cat cake?" Misty asked dreamily, as she lay faceup on the bed, her eyes trying to search the room.

Marco chuckled and said, "We'll save that kitty-cat cake for you to eat later on. You just fainted, *chica!* You scared us amigos to death!"

Michael spoke up, his voice trembling. "What's wrong with her, Marco?"

"When did she last eat a meal with protein?" Marco asked.

Melissa said sadly, "None of us have eaten anything since yesterday."

Marco sighed. "Maria, get some of that string cheese and a handful of peanuts out of my pack. There's nothing wrong with this little girl that some nutritious snacks won't fix."

Misty sat up and peeled strips of string cheese, eating them hungrily between bites of peanuts and sips of boxed apple juice. Once she'd eaten her fill, Marco offered the rest to Michael and Melissa, who accepted it gratefully.

"We've been praying for you all," Maria said gently as she watched her new friends scarfing down the snacks.

"Who has been praying for us?" Michael finally asked after he washed down some peanuts with the juice.

Just then, Jake and Joy appeared at cabin door, looking surprised and confused.

Marco glanced toward Maria, Jake, and Joy, and then answered, "We've all been praying, Michael. All of us."

Jake and Joy, catching on, entered the cabin.

Michael patted his sister's head and looked up at his friends. "I'm sorry I had to lie to you all. I didn't want to, but I was so afraid we'd be taken back to Desert City and split up again. I would ride my bike from school to Whispering Pines Estates, where I'd leave my schoolbooks in the hollow trunk of a tree on an empty lot. That way, Miss Nellie and you all thought I went home to a nice house before coming to work at Miss Nellie's. After work I'd ride over to the Estates to make her think I went home, then when she was gone and Mr. Henley had finished locking up, I'd grab my books and ride back to the art studio, and my sisters would let me in."

The Twiblings all nodded, understanding how afraid the runaways must have been for the past couple of weeks.

"I don't even want to think about what's going to happen to us," said Melissa, her thin body nestled around her young sister's form on the bed quilt. Marco thought they looked like an old-fashioned pen-and-ink drawing from one of Maria's Little House on the Prairie books.

"What's going to happen to you," Marco said in

comforting tones, "is that God's going to make a way for you all to be together, somehow."

"That's right," said Maria. "He loves you all very much."

"But how is He going to help us?" asked Michael.

Marco smiled. "I'm not sure, but I think Miss Nellie has something up her sleeve. When Misty feels up to it, let's head back over to our house. I'll talk to Papa and see if he won't drive us over to Miss Nellie's together."

Michael looked relieved. "Miss Nellie's been so nice to me, letting me sweep up the store for ice-cream treats. I just hate that we stole food from her, but we were so hungry."

"I think she'll understand," Maria said. "In fact, Miss Nellie knows how you all feel."

"She does?" asked Melissa.

"Yes," added Joy, sitting down on the edge of the bed near Melissa and Misty. "She was once a little girl without parents to take care of her too."

"What about the clothes and lunch kit and bi-cycles and stuff we stole from the shopping center outside of town?" Michael asked, worried. "Will we be taken to jail?"

Jake spoke up this time. "If somebody tries to take you to jail, they'll have to get past me first!" He flexed his skinny arms until two muscles, about the size of walnuts, appeared. Now Michael looked extra worried.

Joy laughed. "Don't worry, Michael. It won't all be up to Muscle Man there. Our parents will help us figure out what to do. They are really nice and they love kids. That's one of the reasons they decided to start a Christian camp—so they could help kids!"

Marco suddenly realized how special it was to have two parents who loved him. It was something he almost never thought about. What would he do without his mother and father?

He didn't know, but he prayed that God would be a heavenly Father to his new friends and help them to find a real home—together.

13

GOIN' TO THE CABIN-CHAPEL OF LOVE

Mr. Bigsley, looking very handsome in his dark blue suit, cleared his throat and said, "We are gathered together in this little cabin in the woods, in the presence of God and these witnesses, to join together Nellie O'Brien and Ken Henley in holy matrimony."

Marco couldn't help but feel that Miss Nellie looked like an angel from heaven today, dressed in a flowing wedding gown of soft, white lace. She stared up into the face of her husband-to-be with such love, that Marco secretly hoped that one day he'd have a wife who would love him that much. *A long, long time from now, that is!*

The cabin had been decorated with fresh sunflowers and daisies and baby's breath picked from his mother's garden this fine May morning. Today, the little cabin seemed more like a chapel than a clubhouse—perfect for a wedding as small as this one. Mr. Bigsley, who had once been a pastor before becoming a camp director, had been asked to perform the ceremony.

"And now," Mr. Bigsley said as he motioned three children to move from the back of the room to up front beside him, "Nellie and Ken have asked that you children—Michael, Melissa, and little Misty— join them as I pronounce you one family under the love and leadership of Christ Jesus." Michael took his sisters' hands and started down the aisle. Misty was clutching Miss Nellie's old rag doll close to her side.

Tears of happiness shone on nearly all the faces around the room as they watched the joyful ceremony. Jake and Joy, Mr. Fields, the Garcias, Jamie Klem and her large family, and even Munch-Munch, dressed in a pink jumper, were there. Mrs. Bigsley wore the brightest yellow sun hat that Marco had ever seen. She was soaking tissue after tissue with her joyful tears between playing love songs on a portable piano that Mr. Henley had rented for the day.

Three runaway children, with no home of their own, had found two new parents who wanted nothing more than an instant family brimming with kids. Nellie and Ken had helped the children earn money to pay back the things they'd stolen by letting them work after school in their stores. The girls stayed with Miss Nellie, while Michael stayed with Mr. Henley— until today, when Nellie and Ken would become "Mr. and Mrs. Henley and Family." After the wedding, the new bride and groom could legally adopt all the children as their own.

God, as He so often does, had once again made a way where there seemed to be no way.

And Marco knew, down to the tips of his ratty old tennis shoes, that he was one of the seven richest kids on earth—along with Maria, Jake, Joy, and now, Michael, Melissa, and Misty Henley.

THE TWIBLINGS'
ACTIVITY PAGES

*Always ask an adult to help you
with these crafts and recipes!*

CREATE A CABIN

Use a white shoebox or other
box without a lid as a
cabin and decorate it
on the outside to
look like a log
cabin. (You can
even glue pretzel "logs" on it if you like!) Fill the cabin
with miniature "furniture," using your imagination and
things around your house. For example:

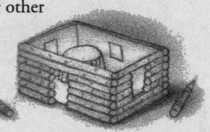

- Thread spools can make little chairs.
- Create a table with paper muffin-tin liners
  turned upside down over a small block.
- Washrags can become "rugs."
- Stickers can make pictures on the wall.
- Buttons can make plates.
- Upside-down thimbles are great cups.
- Scraps of fabric can be cut and glued for
  curtains.
- Miniature books make great beds.
- Single-serving milk cartons and cereal
  boxes can make cabinets and refrigerators.

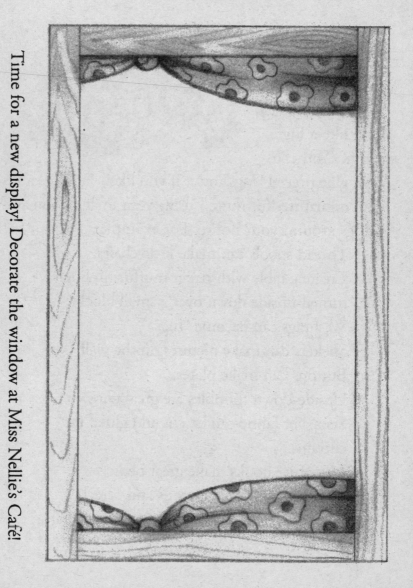

Time for a new display! Decorate the window at Miss Nellie's Café!

HIDDEN ART

Find the missing items in Andy's Art Gallery.

bale of hay	jug of milk	quilt
bicycles	lumber	rag doll
bread	nails	saw
can of tuna fish	peanut butter	

MISS NELLIE'S COCONUT KITTY-CAT CAKE

1 round angel food cake
1 large package vanilla pudding mix
1 medium carton of whipped cream
1 small can of pineapple, drained
M&Ms
thin black licorice
1 cup sweetened coconut
red and yellow food coloring (optional)

With a grownup's help, cut an angel food cake in half so that it looks like two flat wheels with a hole in the middle of each. Stuff the hole of one half with pieces of cake torn off of the other to create a smooth flat surface for the cat face. Cut triangle-shaped kitty-cat ears out of the cake left over and attach them to the cat face with the following fruity frosting!

Frosting: Mix one large package of vanilla pudding mix with one medium carton of whipped cream and a small drained can of pineapple. Spread on cake.

Use two brown M&Ms for cat eyes, and long thin black licorice for cat whiskers. A red M&M can be the cat's nose.

Sprinkle entire cake with one cup of sweetened coconut. (You may also color the coconut orange before sprinkling the cake, if you like, by shaking it in a jar with a drop of red food coloring and six drops of yellow food coloring.)

THE BLESSING GAME

Read the following Bible verse and think about what it means.

> I have learned the secret of being content in any and every situation. (Philippians 4:12, NIV)

Part of learning to be content is being thankful for what we do have, instead of thinking about what we don't have. Play the blessing game! Set a timer for one minute and see how many things you can write down to be thankful for before the buzzer goes off. You can play this alone or with a bunch of friends. Share your list.